D1032236

THE EVERLASTING SNOWMAN

May all your snowman become happy raindrops!!

Hunter D. Darden

By
HUNTER D. DARDEN
Illustrated by Tamara Scantland Adams

Sunflower Publishing
Company

Text copyright © 1996 by Hunter D. Darden
Illustrations by Tamara Scantland Adams
All rights reserved.

Darden, Hunter D.
The everlasting snowman.
[1. Snowmen- Fiction. 2. Everlasting life- Fiction.]
   I. Title
     Easy.
Library of Congress Catalog Number 96-92476
ISBN 0-9653729-0-1

Printed in the United States of America

1st Printing - 1996

2nd Printing - 1997

3rd Printing - 1997

The original watercolor paintings were done on
coldpress watercolor paper.
Separations were made by Color Response,
Charlotte, N.C.
Printed by Signature Press, Statesville, N.C.
Bound by Carolina Bindery, Camden, S.C.

To request additional copies call or fax:
        Sunflower Publishing Company
        704-873-3850 (phone & fax)

In memory of my father, Dr. Council Dudley, a lover of nature.

"For God so loved the world that he gave his only
begotten son that whosoever believeth in him shall not perish but
shall have everlasting life."

John 3:16

Thanks to my sons, John and Tyler,
for the everlasting joy they give me.

Life is always full of pleasant surprises! An unexpected snow was one of nature's gifts to a town of sleeping children. Beautiful snow had blanketed the hills and valleys. Happy children with the day off from school came bounding out of their houses. They were excited about their day of snowy adventures.

The children began the day by sledding down the biggest hills they could find. Making angels in the snow was fun too.

But the best part of all was building the snowman family. They made a mother, a daddy, and a little snowman. They put a funny hat on the daddy, earmuffs on the mother, and a pair of sunglasses on the little snowman.

After a full day of playing, the tired children returned to the comfort of their homes. Everyone was happy while they had their supper by the crackling fire.

Outside the moon was shining brightly on the carpet of new snow.
God's world was calm and beautiful. Nature was at peace.

But, if you listened hard enough, you could hear soft crying. It was the little snowman. He seemed to be very sad even in the midst of all the beauty.

The mother snowman asked, "Why are you crying? You should be happy for it is so nice and cold." The little snowman said, "I'm sad because when our snow melts we won't be here anymore." "Yes we will, said his mother. Our lives will go on forever. Just have faith."

The daddy snowman said, "You need to enjoy your life right now. Just be thankful you are with your family. Be grateful to the person who made you."

The little snowman thought about this for awhile. He began to feel very peaceful inside. He was looking forward to the next day with cheerful thoughts.

In the morning, the sun was shining. Icicles were beginning to drip.
It was going to be a warmer day. The children, still with high spirits,
were headed back to school. They knew there would be more snowy
days in the future.

The little snowman was still happy even as he and his family began to melt. He remembered what his mother and father had told him about life. He knew that something better was waiting for him.

Winter quickly turned into spring. This day had been a lovely one when suddenly gray clouds appeared. Sounds of thunder filled the air. A storm was fast approaching. The children ran inside for shelter from the pouring rain.

The snowman family was together once again! There were signs of the snowmen's presence everywhere in the raindrops! They were nourishing the beautiful spring flowers...

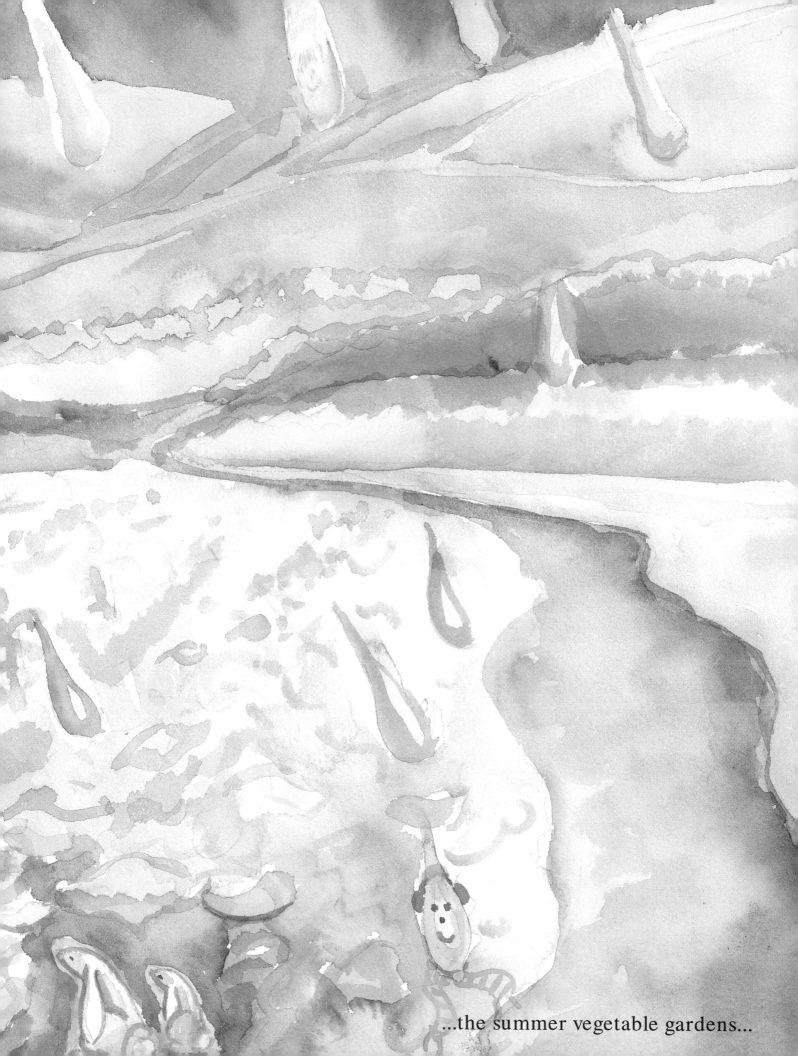

...the summer vegetable gardens...

...and the pumpkin fields in the fall.

The seasons passed and once again winter had returned. Beautiful snow had blanketed the hills and valleys. The children raced outside to build another everlasting snowman family...